The Yin to my Yang

Balance is one the most important virtue in almost anything, be it life or bond. Every bond be it brother - sister or mother - daughter requires balance. This story goes to my Yin, my twin sister who balances me out in every aspect of life.

The Yin to my Yang

Jai Chaudhry

STERLING

STERLING PAPERBACKS
An imprint of
Sterling Publishers (P) Ltd.
Regd. Office: A1/256 Safdarjung Enclave,
New Delhi-110029. CIN: U22110DL1964PTC211907
Tel: 26387070, 26386209
E-mail: mail@sterlingpublishers.in
www.sterlingpublishers.in

The Yin to my Yang
© 2019, Jai Chaudhry
ISBN 978 93 86245 43 4

All rights are reserved.
No part of this publication may be reproduced, stored in a retrieval system or transmitted, in any form or by any means, mechanical, photocopying, recording or otherwise, without prior written permission of the original publisher.

Printed in India

Printed and Published by Sterling Publishers Pvt. Ltd.,
Plot No. 13, Ecotech-III, Greater Noida - 201306,
Uttar Pradesh, India

*THIS BOOK IS DEDICATED TO
MY ELDER SISTER-SANAH DIDI AND
MY TWIN-KHUSHII*

I LOVE YOU BOTH!!

CONTENT

Acknowledgments — vii

A Note on Twins — ix

Chapter 1 - NOSTALGIA — 1

Chapter 2 - A MUCH AWAITED VISIT — 13

Chapter 3 - THE GIFT — 21

Chapter 4 - AN UNEXPECTED TURN — 31

Chapter 5 - #ANOTHERONE — 41

Chapter 6 - PANGS OF SEPERATION — 51

Chapter 7 - GROWN AND FLOWN — 63

Chapter 8 - MIXED EMOTIONS — 73

Chapter 9 - REUNION — 83

Chapter 10 - A WONDERFUL SURPRISE — 93

ACKNOWLEDGMENTS

Special thanks to all those people who acted like a Backbone in making this book possible.

A special thanks to my parents because without their love and support, I would not have been able to follow my dream and passion to write this book. Thank you for always handling my tantrums and supporting my decisions.

I would like to express my gratitude to Pathways school Gurgaon for giving me the wonderful opportunity of stepping closer to my dreams and my mentor Ms Srishti Sagar for critically evaluating my work and guiding me towards the right path.

My sincere thanks to Ms Harleen Kaur Kalra. Without her extraordinary support, this book wouldn't be possible. Thanks for being my friend, mentor and guide throughout my journey.

I would like to thank my Dearest Parul Chachi for a step to step guidance on what I feel has been the most important learning experience of my life. And last but definitely not the least I would like to express my great gratitude and profuse thanks to Dear Vikas Chachu for having the belief, confidence and trust in me to guide and help me in the entire publishing process which has helped me in the culmination of my dreams into reality. THANK YOU ALL FOR BEING A PART OF THIS DEBUT JOURNEY OF MINE

A NOTE ON TWINS

Identical twins – genetically also the same (always of the same gender), identical in appearance/looks.

Fraternal twins – like any other siblings in terms of appearance/looks (can be of same or different gender).

But in both cases, due to shared common experiences and environment while growing up, twins have, by and large, similar personalities / character traits, habits, likes and dislikes, outlook towards life and worldview.

By and large, twins will be on the same side of any argument/discussion. This may imply more in the case of identical as compared to fraternal twins.

With time, changes do take place in personalities, especially if exposed to different sets of external influences like different classes in the same school or different schools, different colleges, different careers, etc.

Most people find it difficult to imagine the special bond between twins. True even for very close relatives like parents, siblings, spouse, etc., who cannot imagine the bond.

Twins understand each other completely, and in most cases, do not need to communicate with each other extensively. Their minds work in the same fashion and they react to similar situations in the same manner even when not together. Example, a similar set of questions attempted in examinations, similar answers. Similar choices made when faced with a set of alternatives.

Since at least in childhood, twins stay together, do things together, eat together, they also, most of the time, fall sick together.

Although with time identical twins also start looking different, throughout life they get used to people staring at them when together.

Innumerable instances of mistaken identities, when one is confused with the other, even by people quite close to both or to one of them. Initially, even parents and other siblings take time to differentiate. Happens in childhood, in school, college, and also later while pursuing their respective careers. Leads to several humorous / interesting episodes in life.

CHAPTER 1
NOSTALGIA

Despite an otherwise warm August, it was a pleasant morning today, thanks to the late monsoon showers that had lashed the city. On this welcoming Sunday morning, I could sense the countless leaves whispering to each other while the gigantic trees in my garden sway gently in the wind and the big buzzing bees swarming in the air in search of nectar. The fragrance of a multitude of flowers, dancing butterflies as they flitted from flower to flower and the chirping of birds made my morning all the more pleasant. The morning seemed so calming, as though I had no cares in the world. Waking up with all the positivity, I threw my favourite Prussian comforter and stretched my hands to reach out to my glasses perched on the side table. Resting next to them was the cup of hot cocoa which Ramu kaka had left about 10 minutes ago, glaring at me with a sarcastic look. Before my milk turned from 'hot' to cold, without further delay I reached out for the mug and then headed for the kitchen to get some biscuits.

As I entered the kitchen, I could see Ramu kaka cooking breakfast of omelette and toast. A short, stocky man, his small round face had wrinkles covering every inch of his skin. His spiky hair once charcoal black were now streaked with silver strands. Mature and with the ability to handle problems wisely, I often turned to him for his good sense and counsel.

"You could have told me to bring the biscuits for you, Sahib. I don't want you to get late for office," Ramu kaka said in a half-scolding manner, as he saw me walk into the kitchen. "Don't worry Kaka, you are not well and today is Sunday anyway, so I have a day off", I said and sauntered back to my room.

Sipping my hot chocolate and munching biscuits, I sat down on my rocking chair, reading the newspaper. 'Ten more killed in Kerala floods', 'Eighteen-year-old killed in bike mishap', 'Trump revoked former CIA Director's Security Clearance'...what's the world coming to, I wondered. Or is it that newspapers prefer to report only negative stories, I pondered. Amidst news of death and destruction, the scenic view from my room overlooking the garden was a soothing balm.

While admiring the blessings of nature, suddenly the study table in my room caught my attention, which was piled with old books and newspapers and was gathering dust. Cleaning it has been in my to-do list for so long I wondered, and then out of all those, my eyes spotted a photo album with torn covers. I reached to it eagerly and started to flip through the memories of my growing up years with my family.

While flipping through the photo leaves, I stumbled upon a picture with which so many memories came flooding back. It was a photograph of my fifth birthday along with my twin sister, Tara, in which we were cutting two separate cakes. Even though our cakes were of the same shape and chocolate flavoured, her's had a floral icing with shades of pink while mine was a typical boyish cake with my favourite cartoon character on it. In the picture, my elder sister looked more eager to blow the candles than both of us.

Reminiscing about the day, I suddenly realised that it was our birthday month, and Tara and 1 will be turning 50 years in just a few days. It's a significant milestone for both of us, as we hit the half-century mark and can now look back at life's experiences, good, bad or in-between with a certain sense of maturity and even wisdom.

It's been five decades since we shared the same womb and were born just 2 minutes apart – Tara entered this world a few minutes after me. Yet then and now we continue to share a deep primeval bond that hasn't waned either with the passage of time or with the different paths our lives have taken. It's a bond that still leaves our friends and families mystified.

Trying to explain scientific things like how twins completely understand each other and have a special language known as 'Cryptophasia' or share everything together has been of little use, as they continue to marvel at the remarkable bond we share even though we no longer live in the same city and don't speak to each other for weeks together, busy as we are with our respective careers and lives. While Tara has been busy working as the head chef department at a five-star hotel in Mumbai, I have remained in Delhi busy managing an export business of my own.

And yet, when we meet there are no hugs or back-slapping. For god's sake, we're twins, and our connection runs much deeper than such outwardly displays of affection. Call it telepathy or whatever, but as Tara always tells her husband – "Ansh, you won't understand, we're twins", to which he simply rolls his eyes with exasperation and amusement.

As the years have rolled by, a lot of things have changed. Tara has a family of her own and is always caught up with some work or the other. Yet, we still manage to Facetime once in two weeks and when we do, our conversation is never-ending. Even though we are fraternal twins, time or perhaps genetics has ensured that we aged similarly. It's funny how our flat stomachs have given ways to rounded bellies and both have similar flecks of grey in our brown hair.

How the years have passed by, I scarcely realised though looking back at them in my middle age now, the first two decades were perhaps by far the best. The sense of abandon and carefree existence that one's childhood brings is seldom to be found in later years. And then came our careers as we settled into our small Delhi flat with our parents, after Dad retired from the Airforce. The house may have seemed small but inside it, lived people with big hearts- a dad full of 'joie de vivre' who believed in seizing happiness whenever it came his way, a soft gentle mother and not to forget our loving elder sister who always felt left out when in the company of 'the twins' as we were often called.

But the house once rocking with laughter and life has gone quiet now as my parents are gone and both my sisters are married and settled with their families, I never married as I spent most of the time taking care of my parents and was too busy establishing my business.

In the album, there were many other photographs of cherished moments which kept on unfolding different memories of different times. One photograph taken during my college days at the Bruce Springsteen rock concert reminded me how I was so overprotective about Tara, following her like a shadow wherever she went.

It just seems like yesterday. Time just flies too fast. We have had a good time while we were young and I do realize that it is in the nature of time to fly leaving us with moments and fond memories.

I was so engrossed in the album that I missed to see a message from my elder sister Neha which said: "*Hey Jaidev, how are you? Its rakhi tomorrow and I will be coming to Delhi to visit you. Tara won't be able to come as she has to attend a meeting which cannot be missed. Although, I will be carrying Tara's rakhi and her special gift with your favourite brownies from Mumbai, let me know if you need anything else, love always, Neha Didi.*"

After reading the message, I couldn't resist the excitement inside me; finally, that time of the year had come. I got up from the chair, kept the album in the cabinet safely, quickly told Ramu kaka to clean Neha's room and ran to take a shower wondering what special gift she would be carrying.

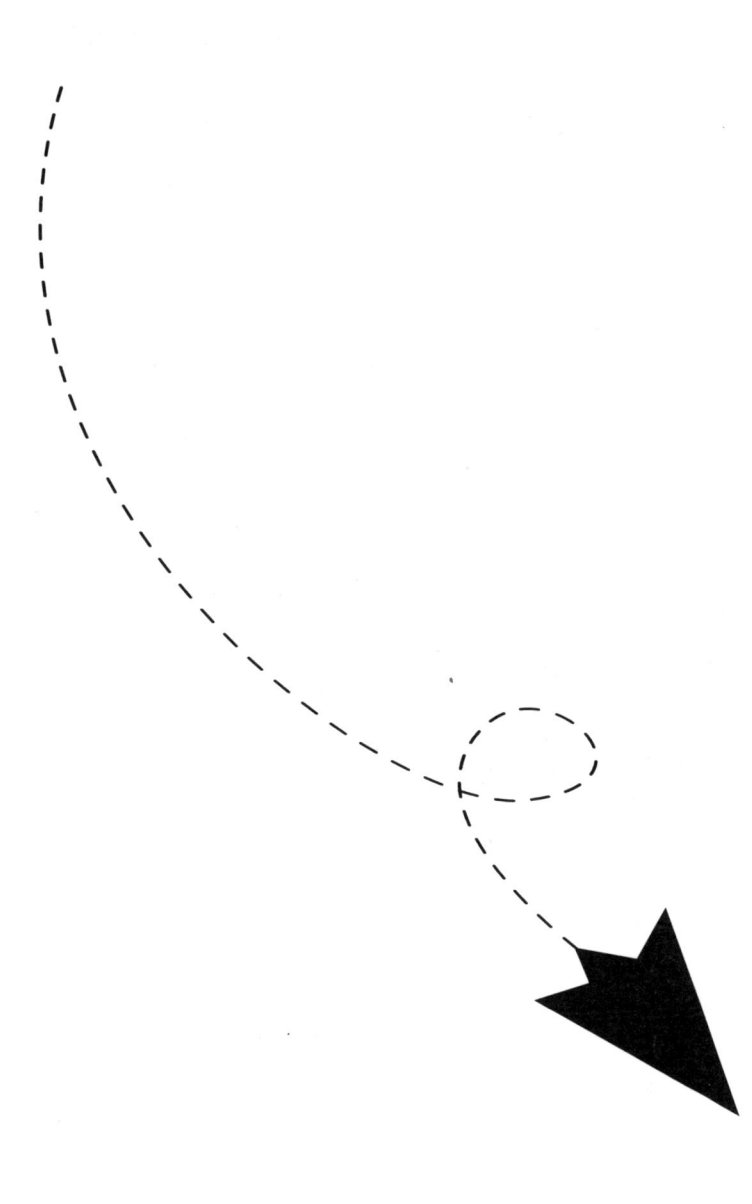

CHAPTER 2

A MUCH AWAITED VISIT

Neha, our sweet, gentle, elder sister is five years elder to us. By virtue of being the first born, she always enjoyed a special place in my parents' hearts, that most first born do, I suppose.

Her overprotective nature hiding behind all her scoldings, her love reflecting in everything she did and still does was really being missed. She was and still is our one-stop solution to all life problems. Despite us being known as the 'thick three', she always had a sense of being left out with me and

Tara. As kids, I recall we had all gone for a picnic and were in the middle of a game of monopoly and Tara and me, started discussing some school cheating matter in our own code language. Even though this dates years back, she still often reminds us of how left out she felt then and still does at times.

In all our fights with her, she used to say, "You twins always single me out in each and every fight of ours and I am left alone".

In spite of the fact that she feels left out, she always went out of her way for us. I still remember when three of us went for a bonding vacation to Bombay where she did her under graduation, her selfless nature and calming presence made us more than comfortable in the chaotic and a completely new environment of Maharashtra.

It had been nearly a year since I last saw her. A busy career as a psychologist and a family to look after made her visits to Delhi a rarity. But this time she told me in advance that she will be flying down to Delhi for a couple of days just to tie me Rakhi. It has been ages since she's been able to do so herself.

Today was the day and I could hardly contain my excitement. Finally, Neha Didi would be coming home after so long. Remembering all those days when the three of us would treat each other to our favourite ice cream from Nirulas with the little pocket money we used to collect, I took the Cordless phone from its cradle and called Ramu Kaka on the intercom to organize all Neha's favourite food. As he picked up the phone, I told him to lay the table and set Neha's room up, to which he replied with enthusiasm "Don't worry, everything is already prepared, you get ready and don't be late for the airport, I am eagerly waiting for Neha madam to come."

To make sure I was on time, I tracked her flight status which said that she would be landing in exactly one hour from now. Without any delay, I quickly got ready, rushed into my car and followed the fastest route to the airport.

So, there I was, waiting impatiently at the arrival lounge for Neha to arrive. And before long, Neha was out, rushing to me and holding me in a tight hug. Poking me in the belly, she said, "Arey, you've put on weight!" I laughed it off saying, "I've reached the 50-mark, didi!" But she insisted that this time she'd prepare a "healthy menu" and ask Ramu kaka to cook my meals accordingly.

"How's Aggu doing? And Ankita?", I asked. Abhimanyu or Aggu for short was Neha's 26-year-old son and Ankita my lovely niece who'd just got married. Aggu, the cricket-crazy nephew of mine was now working with Google in Silicon Valley. And yes, cricket might be an alien sport for the Yanks but Aggu made sure he remained updated with the exploits of Virat Kohli and his team. As for Ankita, who in many ways reminds me of a young Neha, was busy in her newly married life. Now, of course, she is in her family way and the household is buzzing with a cocktail of emotions. Anxiety, excitement, nervousness and joy.

As we drove home from the airport, a feeling of warmth engulfed me as Neha asked me about my work, my health, my friends...and yet I felt something missing. Strange as it may seem, but I was missing Tara being there too. How I wish she'd have been able to make it to Delhi and we could've exchanged notes in our coded language, if only for old time's sake.

CHAPTER 3

THE GIFT

The journey back home from the airport felt shorter as we were so busy catching up that we didn't realize how time flew. While talking to Neha, in some way, I felt connected to Tara; it seemed as if even she was there with us, listening to our chatter. Our chit-chat was endless as we had so many things to catch up, daily lives, families, extended families, health, work, Bombay's weather and a lot more.

After we reached home, Neha got out of the car and started cribbing about Delhi weather like she always did. "It's so hot and humid here, Jaidev, how can you even live here?" she gasped, with a disgusted look on her face. Interrupting Neha, Ramu Kaka came running towards the car, welcoming her to pick her luggage as I escorted her inside the house. "Neha Madam as usual, you are not travelling light, two big suitcases with a heavy cabin bag, that too for just a couple of days. Don't you think it's quite a lot?" asked Ramu kaka as he entered the guest room, wheezing. Leaving the two of them talking, I asked them to excuse me. I went to my room to rest a bit as due to the excitement of celebrating Rakhi with Neha I couldn't sleep well at night.

"Ramu Kaka! After settling Didi, please make me a cup of tea as my head is aching and I want to rest while Didi also freshens up." I was troubling Ramu kaka by saying so, I could make that out from his face.

Approximately two hours later, Didi came out of her room along with a case in her hand. "Sorry if I kept you waiting, I was so tired I took a nap followed by a relaxing shower," she said. "Doesn't matter, Didi! Even I was resting, anyways what's that in your hand", I asked her out of curiosity pointing at the case. "Oh, this is your Rakhi gift, which Tara has sent. She was a little nervous as she wasn't sure if you'd like it."she said, handing me the case. While opening it with childlike excitement, my heart was brimming with emotions and the moment I saw the gift I went speechless for a few seconds. For, never I had imagined that Tara would have kept our childhood belonging so carefully. The gift was a precious one--- it was a pen, the one over which we had fought for good two to three days, as it was a limited-edition one, and owning it was a big deal then.

"Neha Didi, do you remember this pen? I guess we were thirteen or fourteen when dad got this. And asked Tara and me to share it... This pen led to a war between the two of us. I guess that was the only time when we didn't speak to each other for a week. Finally, you along with mom and dad intervened and sorted out the matter." I shared with Neha Didi.

As I held the pen, my body felt very light and so many memories from my teenage years came flooding into my mind. Going down the memory lane, I reminisced how dependent I was on my twin not only for doing my homework but in so many other situations as well. I recall our practical in 7th grade when I was copying all the answers from Tara and the teacher caught me cheating. I still remember what everyone in my school would ask me. "Why are you so dependent on your twin?"

As for my teacher, she would say, "I don't know what will happen to you if something happens to her." Tara was equally dependent on me for her schoolwork as I would write all her essays and comprehensions throughout our school years. The pen also reminded me of the times when we shared the same set of friends in school. We used to hang out a lot together, especially during prom night. Oh, how could I forget prom night. Every year in school we would have a prom night organized for all school students, mainly the seniors. I look back at ours with fondness-- I was so overprotective about Tara that I didn't like it if she talked to boys.

"Why are you behaving like this Jaidev? We are not kids anymore, we are grown-ups and are mature enough to understand that I am a girl and boys will talk to me. If a girl comes and talk to you, I won't feel bad about it," is what Tara would tell me always whenever I intervened while she was talking to any boy.

I would feel bad, or maybe I didn't want to accept the fact that we were teenagers and would have our set of likes and dislikes. I could recollect all the sessions our parents used to have with us to make us understand the common problems all teenagers face and that was *'Adolescence'*. We were told how our body and mind go through various changes during this period.

I never paid much attention to all these discussions. I mean, how can adolescence make me, and Tara have different opinions or feel uncomfortable in each other's presence. After all, we were twins and were together before we even entered this world, sharing the same womb for nine months. But after going through this phase, I realised that even twins cannot get away with this teenage problem and are in many ways like other common siblings.

"Where are you lost?", said Neha Didi. "I know that this pen holds a lot of memories. But now, stop making me feel left out once again. Ramu kaka has called us twice, let's have lunch and then I will tie you Rakhi."

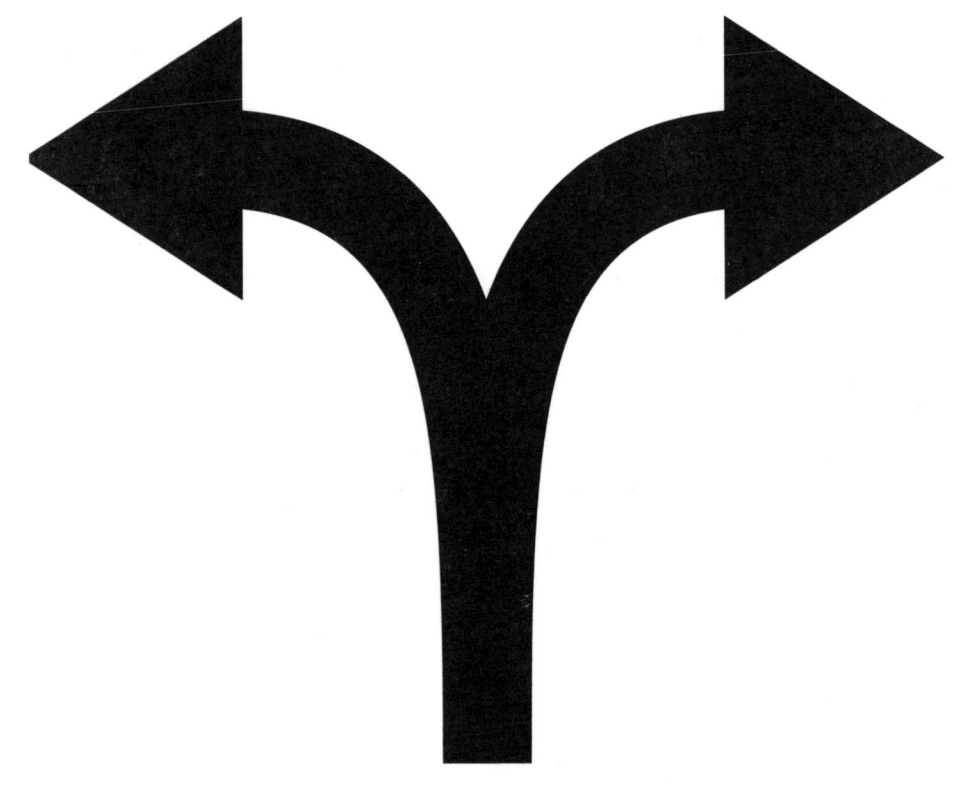

CHAPTER 4

AN UNEXPECTED TURN

As we entered the dining room we saw Ramu kaka busy laying the table. We could sense that he was a little upset with us for being late for lunch. The mouth-watering Dal tadka, Kurkuri Bhindi and Didi's favourite jeera rice filled the room with a strong tempting aroma. "Wow kaka, the taste of your food never changes, in fact, with passing years your food has gone even tastier," Neha praised Ramu kaka's efforts and we could notice his frown turning into a smile.

While enjoying the meal, Didi started talking about Tara and how much she missed her being here too. It felt as if she is reading my mind, but I simply smiled and heard her instead of sharing my thoughts on my twin. "Remember Jaidev, whenever mom used to make these dishes at home, Tara always got upset and we would tease her by saying *'Admit it!! Mom loves us more.'* To this, Tara would retort *'but dad loves me the most'*".

This oft-repeated conversation was firmly etched in my mind. As the conversation carried on, Didi told me that she couldn't help but notice and observe that Tara is omnipresent in all my thoughts and words. I dismissed it outrightly then, but her observation definitely set me thinking. "Is it true?" I asked myself.

Finishing our meal, we picked up our respective cups of cappuccino and walked towards the lawn. Tulsi, our Mali had placed the chairs under the shade of the Gulmohar tree, still leafy but not the dazzling red when its flowers were in bloom. The cool breeze really complimented the aromatic hot coffee. "Jaidev, how can you have your meals alone!" didi exclaimed. "We are not discussing me getting married, not today at least!" I shot back. Pretending to ignore my reply, she continued discussing my possible marriage, this time suggesting the younger sister of her school friend. As soon as she said mentioned, "Mother Teresa School" which was our school name, my thoughts took me back to the days when Tara and I would yell at each other as one of us would inevitably be late getting ready for school delaying the other. With consequences —both being admonished by our teachers. "I am fortunate to have two alumnus at home and don't need to know any other," I remarked, successfully changing the topic. This discussion reminded me that it was a tough phase of my school life when I changed my school in the 9th standard. Both my folks and my school teachers had noticed my increasing dependence on Tara. So eventually, Mom and Dad decided I should switch schools. I was reluctant initially, but Mom and Dad sat me down every day for about 10 days and made me understand their viewpoint. The move to a new school was a tough period for me as I had to leave my friends with whom I had studied since we were tiny tots behind and had to adjust to a completely new environment. But what was far worse was that Tara was no longer around. Each day was a very difficult day for me during this new phase of my life without Tara. Each morning I would sit in the car with a heavy heart because my twin was not there to start my day with and chatter endlessly. In my new school, I missed sharing my tiffin with Tara during the break. In all the lessons I never got bored whenever I was with Tara. Even though we physically attended the lessons, we never paid much attention to the teacher and mentally bunked the lectures most of the time by playing games like *Atlas*. And if we didn't like any teacher, we made phrases in our code language to criticize them. "Neha didi, do you remember the day when Tara and I got the car tyres punctured because we hadn't done our homework and wanted to bunk school, so we bribed our driver by giving him money and to our luck, he accepted it." I confessed to her.

"Oh, yes I do and I also remember that you two got into serious trouble after that! I still wonder how you both managed to get away with doing many such crazy things," she said making a face.

I also remember how cranky I used to get whenever someone asked me "How is your new school going?" because I was completely lost and really felt lonely all the time. After joining the new school, as soon as I reached home, I never greeted my mom and straight away went to Tara's room to share my feelings with her and to tell her how my day went. Tara's situation was far better than me as she still had her old friends around her.

Sitting around the dining table, everyone was curious to know how my day went at the new school but my answer to their questions never changed. "I want to go back to my old school and be with Tara", is what I always told them whenever they asked me any such question.

"Knock! Knock" Neha Didi said, interrupting my thoughts. "Jaidev, it is getting dark, let's go inside so that I can tie you the rakhi. And I hope you remember, you also have to give me my rakhi gift", she said and winked. After didi tied me the rakhi, I quickly went to my room to get her gift. She was very happy to see the limited-edition apple watch I got for her and she said, "Jaidev, as usual, you surprise me every year with your gifts" with sparkling eyes reflecting her joy. I handed over Tara's gift to her- a kindle because she loves reading.

After I handed over the gifts to didi, she took the gifts with her and bided me goodnight. Both of us were in no mood to have dinner, having had a late satisfying lunch. Even I thought of sleeping as tomorrow was another day to be spent with Neha didi and I didn't want to feel tired. I called Ramu Kaka and told him to wake me up by 8 in the morning. As a nightly ritual, I slipped into my bed and started checking office emails on my phone. But still, at the back of my mind, I was longing to meet Tara and relive the happy times we spent together growing up. But I kept them on hold and tried to sleep on time because I often told myself, being swept by sentiments was of no use.

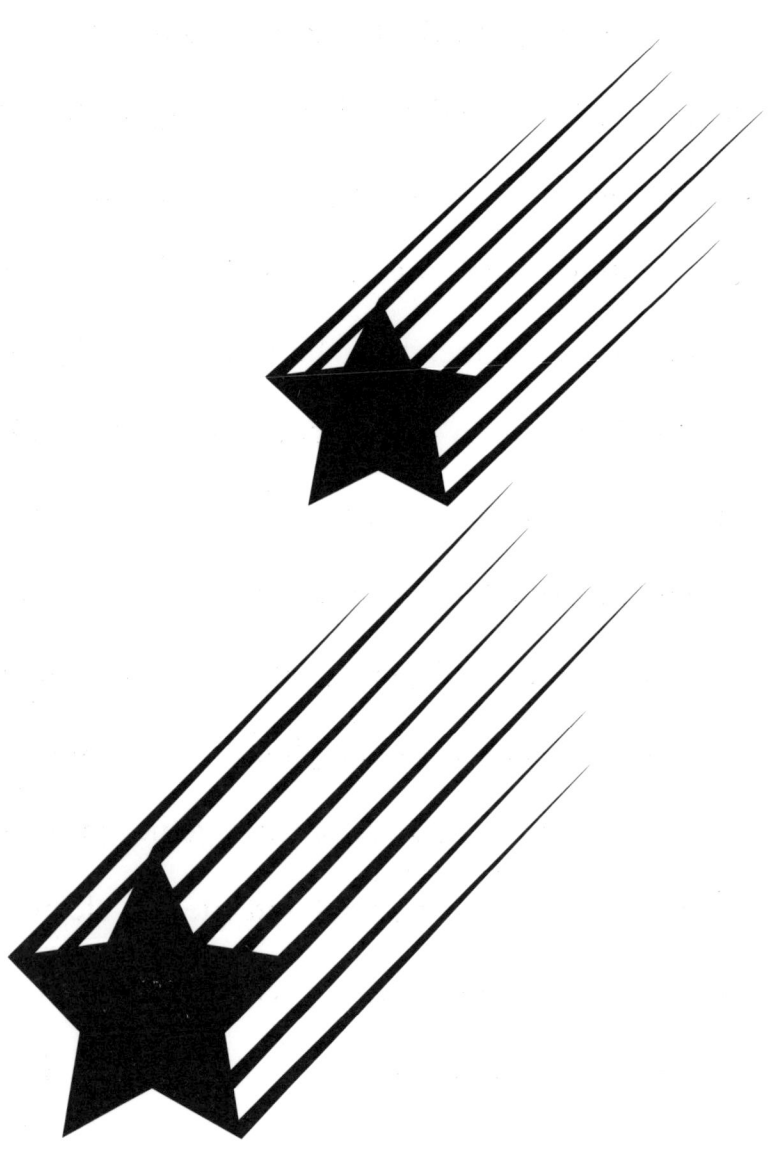

CHAPTER 5

#ANOTHER ONE

*I*t was a lovely new morning; I quickly went to freshen up because I was looking forward to having breakfast with Neha Didi, just like we did every year on the day after rakhi. Reaching the dining hall, I was upset when I saw that the table was not set and breakfast wasn't on the table. I walked into the kitchen to check why there was nothing on the table only to discover Ramu kaka had prepared only my portion of breakfast and was now busy laying it on the same worn out wooden tray he uses to serve me daily.

"Where's Neha's food? Is she still sleeping?" I asked him in a humorous tone. "No Sahib, she has already left for the airport. She tried to wake you up but you were in deep sleep and she didn't want to shake you awake. She has left a letter under your pillow," he said seriously, while I felt my light-heartedness slip away giving way to a sudden heaviness.

I rushed into my room and pulled out the somewhat crushed piece of paper from under the pillow. I moved towards my study to read it in better light near the window through which the sun's morning rays were streaming in. As I unfolded the sheet of paper, many questions cropped up in my mind which seemed to be in a crazy jumble. *"Why did she leave so early? Why didn't she just wake me up? Is there some matter with Tara? I hope everything is fine!"*

Trying to keep these questions aside, I opened the letter. It read:

Good morning Jaidev,

I know you will be annoyed after knowing that I left without even saying goodbye. I received a call from the clinic early morning and have to rush back for an urgent meeting. I tried very hard to get it postponed but nothing worked out. Please, please don't be mad at me and I'll surely make up for this. It's also your birthday tomorrow, Happy birthday in advance. Really sorry to leave you on this day.

I will cherish this time spent with you!!

Love always,

Neha

Despite Neha's explanation and warm words, it left me feeling upset. I felt the same sense of loss I'd felt when Neha had got married. I remember the day and date clearly as if it was yesterday - 16th of October 1992. During all the pre-wedding ceremonies I was very happy for Didi but on the wedding day, I had this sinking feeling within. At first, I couldn't understand the reason but looking at Neha Didi all dressed as a bride, for the wedding made me feel even worse. While everyone was talking about how beautiful my elder sister was looking, my only concern was that she was leaving me. I don't know how but my father could sense my tension so he came up to me and hugged me tightly. I couldn't help but cry quietly, the thought of being separated from Neha leaving me with a sense of utter desolation. "You have to be strong my son, it's a part of life," he consoled me. I remember how Dad then took all five of us to our 'family room' and we did a family hug. This made me feel strong and believe that the bond between us would always keep us united.

The letter also reminded me of another separation--from twin sister Tara who one fine day shared with me her desire to study in Bombay just weeks after Neha's wedding. This news came as a wave of shock to me. My twin sister wanted to leave me and go to Bombay for higher studies. I was very angry with her but after the commitment she made to me that she would write to me at least once a fortnight and keep me updated of all that is happening in her life, I approved of her going to another city for higher studies. I remember each and every word she said to me. "Don't behave like a child Jaidev, it's just a matter of one year and you will not even get to know how this time will pass by," is how she convinced me.

With Neha married and Tara gone for her higher studies, I was all by myself and lonely. No one to watch T.V with, in the evening while eating *Marie biscuits* and gossiping. My days became very monotonous; coming back from my internship, drinking cardamom tea in the evening with mom and dad, watching T.V, at times chatting with friends on the phone till the time dinner was ready and finally slipping into bed was my usual routine after Tara went. In those days, a letter would take two to three days to reach and Tara would inform me in advance on phone whenever she posted one. Everyone could see the excitement of receiving my twin's letter on my face. Her letters were full of emotions and love for me. I still recall one of her letters in which she mentioned the day she bunked her lecture due to the influence of her friends. She was called by the head of her institute and told she would not be allowed to attend lectures for a week as punishment. She somehow managed to not tell either Mom and Dad or Neha didi about this though I could sense her guilt for her action.

During her Diwali vacations, Tara came home for a week. I was thrilled because Neha Didi also came visiting with her husband at the same time. We played cards the whole night and I took a few days off from my workplace, spending time with both my sisters instead. It was like we were back in our school days. Soon the day arrived when Tara had to leave for Bombay but Didi stayed for 2 more days as she could sense my sadness.

That one year when Tara was away was the longest year of my life but I managed to pass it by spending quality time with my parents. It was also during this time that I felt that my mom and dad were growing old physically (mom started to have joint pains) and also mentally (both of them gained a tendency to forget stuff).

"Sahib, your phone is ringing", Ramu Kaka said as he entered the study with my phone in his hand. "I do not want to receive the call as I am in no mood to talk to anybody", I replied in a stern voice. "I can understand that you are missing Neha madam but that doesn't mean that you will neglect your health and not eat anything. Your food is waiting for you downstairs. Please come!!", he said sounding concerned.

CHAPTER 6

PANGS OF SEPERATION

Instead of going to the dining hall, I headed towards the terrace for some much-needed fresh air. Upon reaching it, I saw that the sky was tar black with thick grey clouds dotting it. A feeling of gloom enveloped me with even the skies reflecting my mood. As I sat on my terrace swing, brooding and gripped by a sense of absolute loneliness, I was suddenly overcome by a longing to meet my twin sister, who would always understand my lows without me having to utter a word. Just the look on my face would be enough for Tara to gauge the emotional turmoil that would at times grip me in my struggle to come to terms with my loneliness. My parents while they were around, had always been my support system and helped me fight my seclusion after Tara left for higher studies.

Sipping my cup of hot cocoa, a brew I always had whenever I was in a particularly dark mood, I was overcome with nostalgia. I remembered how my dear parents tried their best to fill the emptiness I felt when Tara was not around showering their endless love. The never-ending sessions of Scrabble I played with them would give me something to look forward to as I'd head home from work. I vaguely remember my mother preparing something special every evening for me to snack on just to uplift my mood. Besides, whenever I entered the house, she'd play a game with me wherein I was supposed to guess what were the evening snacks simply by its aroma. It became a daily ritual which I sort of started enjoying because each and every dish was made keeping in mind what appealed to my taste buds. My parents understood my deep bond with Tara and how immensely I missed her.

I cannot forget the night when dad entered my room while I was busy reading a magazine. I was so engrossed in the article that I realised his presence when he sat on the bed right in front of me.

"Son, do you have two minutes for me", is what he said to start the conversation.

I was taken aback as I was not expecting him to come to my room after dinner. That man to man conversation I had with my Dad that day had created an even more special bond between us. That day on, we started going out for the 'just two of us' dinners though at times mom would accompany us. But mostly, it was just me and Dad, spending time together. I'd tell him how much I yearned for Tara's company as I felt Dad understood me better than anyone else. Dad would hear me out patiently, pointing out on one occasion how our 'twin bonding' left even relatives fascinated. Left under the supervision of our paternal aunt once when Tara and I were in high school, she could see how the two of us were revelled in each other's company, scarcely bothered about engaging with our cousins. When my cousins learnt that Tara had gone for her studies, my dad received calls from many of them expressing their concern for me as they were acutely aware of the fact that Tara and I were inseparable.

It's funny how the bond between twins is apparent to the whole world. After finding out that I had a twin sister, people would always pose questions out of curiosity and would be fascinated with the two of us.

I'd often heard family elders saying that every phase of life is a learning experience and it appeared to be true once Tara had left the city for higher studies and Neha didi was married. It was during this lonesome period that I realised that my relationship with my parents was very strong. It also forced me to realise how tough it was on my parents to raise the three kids, that too with a pair of twins. Twins who'd laugh and cry together, eat together and refuse to do so if the other wasn't eating, refuse to go to sleep if the other wasn't in bed, get into trouble together... the list was seemingly endless.

Our closeness, however, didn't mean that Tara and I never fought. As kids, we'd fight like cats and dogs, even wrestling each other to the ground at times. It was on one such occasion when Tara and I were busy pushing and shoving each other that Dad tried to intervene despite Mom's advice that we best be left alone to sort out things between us. Dad, however, chose not to heed her suggestion and tried to sort out things between us. Only to realise, much to his dismay, that the twins were again thick as thieves and arguing with him instead. For, neither could stand the other being scolded by anyone and their protective instincts would kick in.

"Happy birthday, Sahib!" Ramu kaka interrupted with my favourite cake in his hands, one that he baked every year on my birthday. "Oh, I totally forgot! Is it twelve already?" I asked. "Yes, it is *12:01*", he answered enthusiastically.

"Thank you, kaka!" I said while rushing to take a call on my phone which was now ringing. It was Tara's. After her marriage, it had become a tradition for the two of us to talk every year on our birthday or Facetime to wish each other. So what's so unusual about that, you'd ask. Well, because until she got married, we didn't greet each other on our birthday. For god's sake, we were twins and we didn't need to wish each other. But once she got married, as I said earlier, a new tradition began. The moment I accepted the call, I could hear Tara singing a birthday song for both of us.

"I've won yet again, Jaidev," she said, triumphantly.

And now for the tradition. Every year, Tara and I compete on our birthday to see who will wish the other first.

"Yes, you're always the winner!" I exclaimed.

"Sorry, I couldn't come for RakshaBandhan this year, Jaidev. Neha Didi was really praising you. Anyway, you know Jaidev we talk once in every two weeks but the sheer thrill of calling you on our birthday has never gone. What are your plans for today?" she asked.

"Nothing much, will go to the office in the morning and in the evening some of my friends are coming over for dinner. But I'd really wish that we could've spent our *50th* birthday together. How are you celebrating?" I asked.

"I don't know. The kids are planning something for me for the past two weeks." she said.

"Wow, that's so thoughtful of them. Ok, now let's cut the cake which Ramu kaka has baked for us," I said. And so we did, even though Tara was hundreds of miles away. But we were one soul really. Our usual never-ending conversation followed until Tara said it was time to say goodbye as she was feeling very sleepy.

By then, I'd already received a flurry of birthday greetings messages from nearly everyone in my phone's contact list. The wishes were emotional ones as it was my 50th birthday. After thanking everyone, I decided to turn in for the night. But as I lay on my bed, trying to sleep, I was overcome by a gnawing sense of loneliness yet again. I'd hoped that Tara and I could've spent the day together. But that wasn't possible as both of us had pressing engagements and couldn't fly down to each other's city to be together on this special day.

CHAPTER 7

GROWN AND FLOWN

Feeling restless on my birthday morning, I woke up early and decided to go for a morning walk in a nearby park. I wanted to divert my mind to other things around me to keep a feeling of restlessness at bay. In my agitated state of mind, the beauty of nature helped to feel better. Entering the park through a small gate leading to a narrow path which gradually widened and led to a rolling lawn bordered with old Neem and Jamun trees that muffled the sound of a busy city around them, I tried to calm my frazzled nerves. The quiet environs of the park were occasionally broken by the chirping of birds. Tiny squirrels flitting around too helped lighten my mood.

Walking in the park for an hour and feeling refreshed, I returned home, took a quick shower and got ready for office. I didn't know what was happening to me but I was not at all excited about my *50th* birthday. Finally, I decided to sit in my study to ponder over my present state of mind, still dark and gloomy, before leaving for work.

Tara's wedding album lying on the table caught my eye and I began leafing through it.

"I'm looking so sad. Can't see myself smiling in a single photograph," I said to myself. The album took me on a trip down memory lane--the wedding functions that lasted for three days with Tara super excited and effervescent. And there I was, long faced, indeed sad as my twin was about to leave my side and begin a new life with her husband.

A week prior to her wedding, Tara had demanded that we go out for a coffee, as she wanted to talk to me about the huge transition both of us had to make what with her marriage and her relocating to Bombay. I wanted to avoid this conversation, perhaps because I did not want to face the reality that Tara and I would no longer be each other's shadow--but she requested that we have a chat. And there was no way I could say 'No' to my twin's request.

"Jaidev, I know how you are feeling right now, but marriage is a part of life and we need to live with it. Ansh is a very nice and caring person. He will keep me happy. Oh, come on! Stop looking so morose. We're twins, I say, and nothing can weaken the strong bond we share," said Tara.

"I agree Tara. But is it necessary for you to relocate to Bombay? I mean Ansh can easily set up business in Delhi instead," was my response.

That entire evening went by with Tara trying to convince me that nothing could come between our deep bond. Yet, I simply wasn't able to digest the fact that she was leaving. Finally, Tara called Neha didi and requested her to talk to me. It was only after Neha didi had spoken to me for a good two hours that I realised that I had to accept and live with the fact that Tara was getting married and moving cities. This acceptance was hard, really hard, but I had no choice.

The functions started with the *haldi ceremony* and I still remember that the colour of the day was a vibrant yellow. So everyone wore outfits in this colour. Even I wore a yellow *kurta pajama* - a traditional Indian outfit for boys. Tara looked beautiful in a yellow lehenga and I could gauge from the photographs how happy and excited she looked that day. While her friends squabbled among themselves to apply *haldi* first on Tara. But Tara demanded that I be the first one to do so. I was touched and happy with her gesture. I playfully smeared *haldi* all over her face, leading to much amusement among those present.

"Jaidev, I'm not going to spare you," is what Tara said, chasing me with the bowl of *haldi* paste in her hand.

That evening was full of cheer, with everyone joining in the festivities, the dancing and gorging on the delicious North Indian food.

The following day was the *mehendi* ceremony for which professionals were called, they wove intricate patterns with the *mehendi* on the hands of all women at the ceremony. The entire evening, I was busy catering to the needs of my relatives but deep down inside my heart, the feeling of the impending separation from Tara was building up. I was smiling and pretending to enjoy the function so that Tara and Neha didi wouldn't come to know how heavy and sad my heart felt. The entire evening went by with Neha didi and Tara performing to various dance numbers and everyone enjoying to their heart's content.

And then dawned the day which I so wanted to avoid--it was *Tara's wedding day!!!!* Going through the album I remembered how I was no longer able to hide my real emotions from my family. They could see that my eyes were watery and I was avoiding any sort of conversation with everyone. Neha didi tried a lot to cheer me up but it was of no help.

I clearly remember barging into the room where Tara was getting ready. I demanded a little privacy with her and asked all others present to leave the room except for Neha didi who was allowed to stay.

"Tara I cannot take it anymore," is what I said with tears rolling down my eyes.

"Jaidev, please don't do this. Even I'm feeling very bad," Tara said with tears rolling down her cheeks too.

After hearing her say these words I left the room without uttering another word.

The album also contained images of Tara's *bidai* where everyone was seen crying especially me. I could see my father and mother crying while hugging Tara. I recall how I couldn't bear it anymore and rushed towards my room without even saying a bye to Tara. Neha didi came running me and hugged me tightly.

This rush of memories only made me feel more miserable so I closed the album and without wasting any more decided to head to work. Before leaving I asked Ramu kaka to prepare dinner for 10 people as my close friends were coming to celebrate my 50th birthday with me. But in my heart of hearts, I really wasn't looking forward to the celebrations.

CHAPTER 8

MIXED EMOTIONS

As I reached the office, I was greeted with bouquets and the entire office was decorated with streamers and balloons. A chocolate cake with 'Happy fiftieth' written on it in white icing lay waiting on a table in the middle of the vast reception with the entire office staff standing around it, bursting into a birthday song for me as soon as I entered. I felt honoured and respected. Entering my cabin, I saw a pile of gifts on my desk that took me back to the birthday celebrations I would have with Tara during my school years. Dad would host a massive themed birthday party for us every year and dozens of people were invited including relatives and friends, both from school and our colony. The number of gifts we received would later be stacked in a pile and kept in our playroom. Tara and I had made it a tradition of sorts--we would take a day off from school the day after our birthday simply to unwrap dozens of gifts. Fortunately for us, our parents never scolded us for taking leave from school on that particular day. Instead, they would join us as each gift was unwrapped and then examined with much glee.

One year, while we were going through the gift unwrapping ritual, Mom shared with us the fact that she was terribly nervous and scared when she first discovered that she was expecting twins. Dad and my grandparent's excitement and fascination for twins though knew no bounds as we were the first set of twins in the family. The fact that twins were on the way ensured a permantent smile on my Dad's face that never faded, our Mom shared with us.

"May I come in sir! Sorry to disturb you but I just wanted to discuss today's meetings with you," my assistant, Seema said while standing near the door.

"Yes Seema, but please cancel all my meetings post 5 pm as I have to leave early today." I told her.

"Ok sir, happy birthday once again," she said while leaving the room.

The afternoon passed quickly with people streaming to wish me and make me feel special. By 4.30 pm I'd left the office and headed home. Reaching home, I made sure everything was neat and in place, the table set and the glasses for drinks arranged neatly. I was expecting my guests around 6 p.m. and decided to choose what I would wear from my well-stocked wardrobe. As I stood in front of the open cupboard, figuring out what to wear, an old photograph of Tara and me with her family after marriage tumbled out from a lower shelf. Looking at the photograph, a wave of not so happy memories flooded my mind. Sitting on my rocking chair, I recalled how Tara's behaviour changed--at least I thought so--after marriage. In the initial few months of her marriage, she would call me two to three times in a fortnight. But gradually, the frequency of these calls reduced to just one call a month. This made me feel depressed and irritable and I found myself snapping for no reason and at everyone. Growing more and more detached, I found myself avoiding family functions and always in a bad temper. Even my parents really missed Tara but they knew that it was in our culture for every girl to get married and live with her husband in a separate house, on the contrary, my feelings for Tara was different than my parents and I missed her more because she was my twin and no one could understand the strong bond we shared.

I decided to call Tara to confront her because of her changed behaviour but she did not answer the call, instead, her husband, Ansh picked up the landline. I spoke to him in a mellower tone and asked for Tara. After all, I wasn't so close to him as I was to Tara and I had no intention of sharing with him the separation pangs I felt since she was married.

A few days later, Tara called me and for a few seconds, neither of us spoke. The silence was finally broken by my sobs. A worried Tara demanded the reason for this behaviour on my part. The phone conversation we had that day is still as clear as daylight to me even after all those years.

"Jaidev, what happened? You are making me worried," said Tara in a serious tone.

"You'd promised me that you'd keep calling regularly but did you live up to your promise? Have you forgotten me?" I asked. "What's happened now, no answer?" I continued.

"You are taking it in the wrong spirit, it's nothing of this kind. Life after marriage is very different. I have so many responsibilities on me now." Tara said defending herself.

"I don't care! You assured me that you will not change after marriage", I said angrily.

Tara got really annoyed and started scolding me. I was taken aback with this behaviour of hers.

"Sorry for shouting at you Jaidev but you need to understand that we are no longer teenagers. Now I have a family to look after. Aren't you happy for me that I am married to such a nice and caring boy? Ansh is very protective about me; he's heads over heels in love with me and never misses an opportunity to express his love for me. Your twin is very happy, so shouldn't you be happy too?" asked Tara as she tried to reason with me.

Her remarks made me realize that I was troubling everyone around me and most of all Tara with my childish behaviour. And that I needed to grow up and behave like a mature, grown-up man. I apologized to Tara and assured her that I would no longer behave in such a petulant manner anymore. Relieved at my mood change, she broke some happy news to me--that she was expecting and soon I was to become an uncle.

"Jaidev! What are you doing inside? Come out!", my friend Rahul said while knocking at the door of my room.

"Just give me fifteen minutes, I'm coming out." I replied while keeping the picture back inside the cupboard.

I dressed up quickly and went to the living room where some of my friends were already waiting for me. The moment I entered the living room, they broke in 'Happy birthday to you….'. The warmth of my friends had enveloped me in a happy glow.

CHAPTER 9
REUNION

"Let's head towards the dining area and start the celebrations," I suggested.

As I entered the dining room, I noticed the window curtains and the dining table too had new tablecloth spread over it. The aroma of scented candles added to the ambience, making it even more pleasant and relaxing. All my friends were full of praise for Ramu kaka who had put in all this effort to make the evening more enjoyable. Inquiring about the new curtains, Ramu kaka confessed that it was Neha who had given him the money to buy new curtains as she knew very well that I would never do it. The candles were a birthday gift from Ramu kaka and I was touched by these caring gestures by both didi and kaka.

Ayaan, one of my friends handed me the bottle of champagne to open while the rest of them were busy chatting and joking among themselves. Catching sight of the champagne bottle, my mind flitted back to exactly a quarter of a century ago. It was our 25th birthday party and Dad popped open the Champagne and offered Tara and me a glass each of the bubbly. It was the first drink we had ever had in the presence of our parents.

"Wish you a very happy birthday Jaidev! Cheers!" said my friends, as they hugged me.

I poured champagne into the glasses and served it to everyone. "Cheers to our friendship!!!" as we raised a toast to each other and started our never-ending conversation. It was a happy gathering of friends who'd known each since school. There was a sense of easy camaraderie as we chatted about our work, families, movies, music, cricket and yes, food.

"How's Tara?", Ayaan asked me out of curiosity.

"She's very happy in her life but envies me as I get to meet you all but she cannot because of the distance. Whenever we facetime, she makes sure to ask about each one of you," I replied placing my glass on the table.

"Jaidev, remember the day when Tara scolded you in front of the girl you liked the most because you hadn't had your medicine. We made so much fun of you that day but not to forget how protective she was about you and always acted as a shield whenever you faced any problem. I always wished that I had a twin sister like her", said Rahul in a nostalgic tone. "She really missed you after you shifted to another school and started spending recess time in her class alone," Rahul continued.

"Rahul, it's a scientifically proven fact that twins have a very strong connection unlike other siblings. The pain of separation is very evident to anyone and everyone around us and what do you think---that I was fine moving to another school without my twin? It took me months to adjust to that school," I replied while feeling emotional.

"Even the teachers were aware of the strong bond Tara and you shared and were always fascinated with the two of you," said another friend Aisha.

"Why aren't you all eating? Rahul your glass is still not empty. Come on guys what's the matter! It's my 50th birthday, show some enthusiasm," I blurted out.

By diverting attention to the drinks, I just wanted to end the discussion about Tara and me. I wanted to avoid talking about the days that Tara and I spent together as I didn't want to feel the pain of separation anymore. So seeking to change the topic, I began talking about the hurdles I was facing in my export business due to a recent change in government regulations and my plans to expand it.

"I am planning to open a branch of my export business in Hong Kong. I'm trying to make links over there so that I can understand and study the market well. Please let me know if anyone of you can help me in this," as I attempted to divert everyone's attention from Tara and me.

"That's amazing! I have links with a few people in Hong Kong because of my business. I'll connect with them and I am sure they will be of some help to you," said another friend, Ajay. "Also, let's celebrate New Year's Eve together this year. We'll invite Tara as well and it will be like a school reunion, just like the one we had 12 years ago," he suggested.

"Oh! Just don't mention that day as all of you played a prank on me by fooling me into going into the ladies washroom. Even Tara was part of the prank," said Ayaan sounding annoyed even after so many years. Everyone was in splits recalling the prank and Ayaan's misery that day.

"That was one fun-filled day when we all behaved the way we used to during our school days. Ayaan you didn't talk to us for a good one month after that because of the prank," said Rahul while reminding us all of the good old days.

It was an evening of warmth and laughter and I was in a happy frame of mind. As time ticked away, I asked Ramu kaka to serve the food. But my friends would have none of it. They simply wanted to continue with the snacks and drinks while demanding that we play old Hindi melodies. Suddenly, Ajay stood up and started singing along with the number that was playing. He pulled me to the dance floor and in a short while, all my friends were shaking a leg with even Ramu kaka joining in. I could sense how my friends were making a special effort to make my fiftieth birthday a special and memorable one. They were not just friends, they were family.

Around 9.30 pm while we were all dancing and enjoying ourselves, the doorbell rang. I was puzzled for a moment as I wasn't expecting any more guests. Or had the neighbours come to complain about the loud music, I wondered.

"Who could it be at the door?" I mused while calling out to Ramu kaka to go and check who was at the door.

CHAPTER 10

A WONDERFUL SURPRISE

"Sahib, can you please open the door as I am busy in the kitchen", Ramu Kaka requested.

I was stunned because Ramu kaka has never behaved like this earlier. Giving him a benefit of doubt because of his age, I didn't react and headed towards the door to open it. The moment I opened the door, I saw a group of people with their backs facing towards me.

'SURPRISE!!!!'

The sight left me overwhelmed and I couldn't believe my eyes. For a minute I thought I was dreaming but the reality was that my entire family including my twin sister Tara was standing in front of me.

"Tara!! Neha Didi!! How come you all.... I'm short of words and I don't even know what to say", I revealed my emotions with watery eyes.

"How was the surprise, did you like it? Neha Didi asked out of excitement.

"Like it! I can't even express my feelings right now. This is the best birthday gift ever. I said while tears rolling down my eyes.

"Happy birthday to us Jaidev. Sorry, I know that you must be feeling terrible the whole day, but wasn't it worth the wait?", Tara asked.

"Happy birthday Jaidev uncle." Veer, Tara's son wished me with enthusiasm.

"Will you take us inside or are we celebrating your birthday standing here only", Neha said.

After reaching the dining room, the secret was revealed that Neha Didi left me so that she could plan the surprise and everyone present in the room was a part of this including my friends and Ramu kaka. For the same reason Ramu kaka didn't open the door and my friends were refusing to eat dinner. I felt so loved that minute that I didn't even know how to react. I realised that my family and friends were so concerned about me and made my 50th birthday so special and memorable. Tara, my twin whom I was missing immensely was standing right in front of me. I am grateful to God for being so kind on me and keeping my loved ones close to me on my 50th birthday.

"Jaidev come let's cut the cake. I have got your favourite flavour", Tara said, placing the cake on the table.

Tara and I cut the cake while everyone was singing for us. "I love you Jaidev and you don't know how much I miss you each day. No one will understand the inseparable bond we share and never ever think that my love will change for you", Tara said with a heavy voice and watery eyes.

"Let the party begin!" Neha Didi exclaimed while making Sangria.

Everyone started dancing on the latest Bollywood songs while I was standing in one corner sipping my Sangria and watching my family and friends enjoying our birthday. This was the time when I observed Veer who was sitting on a chair and eating snacks. He used to come every year with Tara till his school years but once he entered college he didn't come because he was too busy with his friends and studies. I decided to walk towards Veer and chat with him.

"How are you Veer? You are looking very handsome", I initiated the conversation.

"I am great! Thank you so much. I hope you liked the surprise. Mom was planning this with Neha *masi* from almost a month", Veer replied.

"I loved the surprise. My birthday couldn't have been better than this and thank you so much", I said.

While talking to Veer, Tara came and stood next to us as she wanted me to dance with her. But after listening to our conversation she decided to add on to it.

"You know that I was the mastermind behind this plan. I wanted to give you a very big surprise and make our 50th birthday as special as I could. Dear brother you know I have another surprise for you and that one will make you jump", Tara exclaimed with enthusiasm.

"I cannot thank you enough! I would have never thought that you all will make this day so special for me. I love you all so much", I acknowledged. "Now I am very curious to know the other surprise as well. Please tell me", I continued talking.

"No, not at all! You have to wait till the time Ansh comes. I want to disclose the surprise in his presence, till that time you need to keep patience", Tara said, pulling me to the area where everyone was dancing.

My excitement saw no boundary and I started dancing along with my friends, sisters and my nephew. After almost 20 minutes of nonstop dancing, I headed towards the table to drink some water, to catch up with my breath and there I saw my favourite *hot chocolate fudge from Nirulas* with a label on it, which read:

'For my loving brother'

From Neha Didi

It tasted exactly the same as it used to when we three siblings treated each other with the little pocket money we collected during our childhood days. Suddenly everything started to seem so perfect with my loved ones around me.

"I hope you loved it. Tara and I have made sure to give you everything you love and cherish on this occasion of your 50th birthday. You know that me and Tara meet quite often as we stay in the same city but it's you who is left out because of the distance", Neha Didi explained while expressing her love and affection for me.

I hugged her tightly for good 2 mins.

"Happy Birthday Jaidev!", a voice said from behind. On turning around, I saw Ansh standing with a bottle of wine in his hand.

"Thank you so much!", I replied while shaking hands with him.

"Sorry I got late. The meeting I was attending extended for 2 hours", Ansh said.

"MEETING? IN DELHI? How come? Your business is in Bombay, so how come you were having a meeting here in Delhi", I asked with a puzzled expression on my face.

"That's was the other surprise I was talking about. Jaidev, we are shifting permanently to Delhi!", Tara revealed while expressing her joy.

Ansh is expanding his business and opening a new branch here. He will be travelling to Bombay often but Veer and I will stay in Delhi only", Tara continued talking.

I wanted to jump in excitement but I couldn't because of so many guests and of course my age, instead I hugged Ansh.

"Tara had a similar reaction, Jaidev. Every year on our anniversary she would request me to shift to Delhi so that she can be with you", Ansh concluded.

I cannot ask for more on this day. "Seriously, thank you from the bottom of my heart", I addressed the gathering.

"Neha madam, your phone is ringing from the past half a minute", Ramu kaka said while handing the phone to Didi.

The expressions on Neha Didi's face made it evident that something big has happened. We all were looking eagerly at her as we wanted to know the reason for the same.

"Ankita has been blessed with fraternal twins – a boy and a girl", Neha Didi exclaimed with excitement.

Everyone in the room shouted with enthusiasm. I could feel a shiver run down my spine, not of fear but an absolute delight. I wanted to let out a hurrah! But felt a catch in my throat. Was it only because I was thrilled with the arrival of twins? Or was it because I feared the new arrivals would have to go through the pangs of separation, just as I did long years ago. But that's a small price to pay for the sheer good fortune of having a twin. The ice to my cream, the sugar to my spice, the yin to my yang.